Patagonia Clatterbottom is the head teacher of Pirate School.

She has a secret cupboard full of food . . .

. . . and Smudge, Flo, Ziggy and Corkella want to eat it!

D0181244

Jeremy Strong once worked in a bakery, putting the jam into three thousand doughnuts every night. Now he puts the jam in stories instead, which he finds much more exciting. At the age of three, he fell out of a first-floor bedroom window and landed on his head. His mother says that this damaged him for the rest of his life and refuses to take any responsibility. He loves writing stories because he says it is 'the only time you alone have complete control and can make anything happen'. His ambition is to make you laugh (or at least snuffle). Jeremy Strong lives near Bath with four cats and a flying cow.

Books by Jeremy Strong

GIANT JIM AND THE HURRICANE
THE INDOOR PIRATES
THE INDOOR PIRATES ON TREASURE ISLAND
MY BROTHER'S FAMOUS BOTTOM
MY DAD'S GOT AN ALLIGATOR!
MY GRANNY'S GREAT ESCAPE
MY MUM'S GOING TO EXPLODE!
THERE'S A PHARAOH IN OUR BATH!

PIRATE SCHOOL – JUST A BIT OF WIND
PIRATE SCHOOL – THE BIRTHDAY BASH
PIRATE SCHOOL – WHERE'S THAT DOG?
PIRATE SCHOOL – THE BUN GUN
PIRATE SCHOOL – A VERY FISHY BATTLE

Jeremy Strong
Pirate School

The Bun Gun

Illustrated by Ian Cunliffe

PUFFIN

This book is dedicated to Cameron Bierman

PUFFIN BOOKS

Published by the Penguin Group
Penguin Books Ltd, One Embassy Gardens, 8 Viaduct Gardens, London, SW11 7BW, England
Penguin Group (USA) Inc., 375 Hudson Street, New York, New York 10014, USA
Penguin Group (Canada), 90 Eglinton Avenue East, Suite 700, Toronto, Ontario, Canada M4P 2Y3
(a division of Pearson Penguin Canada Inc.)
Penguin Ireland, 25 St Stephen's Green, Dublin 2, Ireland (a division of Penguin Books Ltd)
Penguin Group (Australia), 707 Collins Street, Melbourne, Victoria 3008, Australia
(a division of Pearson Australia Group Pty Ltd)
Penguin Books India Pvt Ltd, 11 Community Centre, Panchsheel Park, New Delhi – 110 017, India
Penguin Group (NZ), 67 Apollo Drive, Rosedale, North Shore 0632, New Zealand
(a division of Pearson New Zealand Ltd)
Penguin Books (South Africa) (Pty) Ltd, Block D, Rosebank Office Park, 181 Jan Smuts Avenue,
Parktown North, Gauteng 2193, South Africa

Penguin Books Ltd, Registered Offices: One Embassy Gardens, 8 Viaduct Gardens, London, SW11 7BW, England

puffinbooks.com

First published 2005
009

Text copyright © Jeremy Strong, 2005
Illustrations copyright © Ian Cunliffe, 2005
All rights reserved

The moral right of the author and illustrator has been asserted

Set in Times New Roman
Made and printed in China

British Library Cataloguing in Publication Data
A CIP catalogue record for this book is available from the British Library

ISBN 978-0-141-31926-1

Contents

1. Top-Secret Food

CHOMP! CHOMP! SLURP! SLURP!

What was that noise?

It was lunchtime at Pirate School and the teachers were in the head teacher's cabin, eating. Mrs Muggwump was chomping a jammy doughnut.

Miss Fishgripp and Mad Maggott were slurping champagne. Glug! Glug! Glug! Miss Snitty, the secretary, was eating a lettuce leaf. (She was on a diet.)

But the noisiest eater was the head teacher, Patagonia Clatterbottom. She sat in her boat-pram, eating a great pile of food. She had one big sausage, two fried eggs, three bits of bacon and at least four hundred baked beans.
SHLIPP! SHLURPP! BURRPP!

What were the children eating?
Ziggy was eating a single baked bean.
Corkella was eating a baked bean.
Smudge and Flo were each eating a
baked bean. Even Jazz the dog was
eating a baked bean. It was a very
small lunch.

"I'm hungry," moaned Ziggy.

"We're all hungry," grumbled Corkella.

"Woof," said Jazz.

Smudge peered through the keyhole into Patagonia's cabin. "They're drinking champagne!" he cried.

Little Flo peered through the keyhole. "Have you seen their food store? It's wonderful," she sighed.

It was wonderful too. Patagonia's cupboard was bursting with yummy-scrummy food.

Ziggy banged on the door.
"What do you want?" roared
Patagonia. "You horrible little prawn!"

"We want food like yours," said Ziggy, very bravely.

"Ha! No chance!" bellowed Patagonia Clatterbottom. "This is for staff only. Get back to your baked bean, and don't eat it all at once." She slammed the door – BANG!

2. The Woppagobs

The children were not the only ones who knew about the food. Boris Bigbelly and Fifi Foh-Fum were grown-up pirates, but they didn't steal treasure – they stole food. They were the fattest pirates ever, and their gang was called the Woppagobs.

Boris Bigbelly

Fifi Foh-Fum

Lilly Lollop

Two-Tooth Charlie

Boris and Fifi had been watching
Patagonia Clatterbottom doing her
shopping. They knew she was the head
teacher of Pirate School. But they
didn't know where she kept all the food
she was loading into her boat-pram.

"I shall find out," said Fifi Foh-Fum.
"I shall have an accident-on-purpose."

"I'm so sorry!" cried Fifi. "Let me help you. What a lot of food you have! Your children must eat an awful lot."

"Nonsense!" roared Patagonia Clatterbottom. "This is for staff only. I lock it away in my Top-Secret Food Store. Otherwise the children would eat it before you could say 'strawberry ice cream with chocolate chips and gravy'. Ha!"

Fifi hurried back to Boris. "That potty Patagonia likes gravy on her ice cream. But guess what! I know where she keeps the food!"

Boris grinned. "Excellent! We'll meet the gang at our secret cave and make a plan."

"When it's dark we shall creep up to their ship," said Boris.

"Creep, creep, creep," went Lily.

"Why did you say that?" asked Boris.

"I'm doing sound effects," Lily explained.

"And then we'll tiptoe to Patagonia's cabin."

"Tippy-tippy-tippy-toe," said Lily. Boris rolled his eyes.

"And then we burst in –"

"RAAAAAAAARGH!!"

All the pirates fell off their chairs.

"Was that another sound effect?" demanded Boris crossly.

"Yes, and very effective it was too," said Lily.

Boris picked himself up from the floor. "Just make sure you follow the plan," he snarled. "We burst in, smash open the cupboard and snatch all the food."

"And then we eat it," said Fifi.

"Exactly. Chomp chomp chomp. Jumping jellyfish! Now you've got me doing it, Lily!"

3. Smudge's Plan

Back at Pirate School, Smudge had come up with a plan to get the food too.

"We stand by the door and shout, 'Fire! Fire!' The teachers will rush out and I shall slip inside and raid the food cupboard. What do you think?"

Little Flo was amazed. "You are clever," she told him, and they both blushed.

"Good plan," agreed Corkella. "It might just work."

"Woof," went Jazz.

So they stood outside the head teacher's door and yelled, "FIRE!!!"

"Fire!" bellowed Mad Maggott, charging out of the cabin.

"Fire!" squeaked Miss Snitty before she was mown down by Mrs Muggwump and Miss Fishgripp as they made their escape.

"Fire – oooh – aargh – help!" went Patagonia Clatterbottom as she tripped over Miss Snitty and went tumbling along the passage.

Smudge dashed into the empty cabin and raced to the Top-Secret Food Store. He pulled out buns and doughnuts galore. Then he made a dash for safety, straight into Patagonia Clatterbottom, who was struggling up from the floor.

"What's this? A piddly piffling pirate, being piratical in my pantry!"

Uh-oh! He's in big trouble now!

"Throw him in the hold!" cried the head teacher.

As Smudge was dragged away Ziggy reached out and stuffed something down the back of Smudge's trousers.

"Oh!" said Smudge, very surprised.

"Shhh," whispered Ziggy, with a wink.

Mrs Muggwump opened the hatch and Miss Fishgripp dropped Smudge inside. Bang! The hatch was shut tight.

It was so dark in the hold that Smudge couldn't see a thing. He felt inside his trousers. What had Ziggy put there? A torch. Clever Ziggy!

Smudge switched on the torch and began to explore. There wasn't much in the hold at all. He found a few old tools

and a table. He met several friendly rats too.

That's a very big rat.

But it hasn't got a tail!

But he couldn't find any way out.
Smudge sat down and wondered what
to do next and that was when he heard
muffled voices from above.

Smudge listened carefully. He heard someone say, "Get the gangplank ready. Tomorrow we shall make that wretched child walk the plank!"

Smudge was very scared when he heard this, but he realized he was right

beneath Patagonia's cabin, and that
gave him another idea, an even
better one.

4. The Pirates Strike

Boris Bigbelly stood at the back of the little rowing boat. "This has got to be a big surprise. We mustn't wake anyone on board, so don't splash."

"Splish, splish," whispered Lily.

"I said no splashing!" hissed Boris.

"I wasn't. I was splishing," said Lily. "And that's a lot quieter."

The rowing boat rocked gently up against Pirate School. All was quiet. (Except for Patagonia, snoring.) The Woppagobs threw ropes on to the deck and then they climbed up them.

"Tippy-tippy-toe. Creak!" went Lily
as they crept across the deck.

"Be quiet!" muttered Boris.

"I'm pretending there was a loose
plank. It makes it more exciting."

"No more sound effects! Right, this
is Patagonia's cabin. Get ready – on the
count of three, OK? One . . . two . . .

. . . THREE! CHARGE!!"

Uproar! The teachers woke with a start and hurried to Patagonia's cabin.

"Gerroff!"

"Argh!"

"Take that!"

"No, you take THAT!"

"Woof! Grrrr!"

"Ow!"

In a few moments the Woppagobs
had won the fight.

"Now we're going to steal all your
food," sniggered Fifi Foh-Fum.

"You'll never get away with it,"
growled Patagonia.

"I think we will," sneered Boris,
opening up the Top-Secret Food Store.

Miss Snitty peeped into the cabin.

What a pickle the pirates were in!

"Oh yummy yums!" chorused the
Woppagobs, staring at the gorgeous
pile of food. And then, just as Boris
Bigbelly reached in to grab it all . . .

Whoooooosh!

The food vanished right in front of
their eyes!

5. Smudge's Surprise

Down in the hold Smudge had been working on his clever plan. He had found a little saw and made a hole right beneath the food cupboard. Smudge heard the fight, but had no idea what was going on. Then, just as the pirates tried to grab the food, Smudge finished the hole and the food fell straight down into the hold.

"That little kid's nicked our food!"
cried Fifi, staring down the hole.

"It's *our* food," snarled Patagonia.

"Boo hoo!" sobbed Lily.

"Is that another sound effect?" frowned Boris.

"No. I'm upset. Our food's gone! Boo hoo!"

"I'm going to get it back," declared Boris, and he jumped down the hole.

Of course, he was far too fat and he got stuck like a cork in a bottle. SPLOP!

"Help!" he squeaked.

Fifi Foh-Fum pulled and pulled. Lily Lollop grabbed Fifi, and Two-Tooth Charlie pulled on Lily. But it was no good. Boris was well and truly stuck.

All that banging and crashing had woken up the children. Miss Snitty tiptoed to their room.

"I don't know what to do," she wailed.

"Don't worry," said Corkella, holding her hand. "We do! We're pirates!"

They crept down the passage and found everyone in Patagonia's cabin, with Bigbelly stuck in the hole.

They quickly shut the door. Now the Woppagobs were their prisoners. (And so were all the teachers!)

BANG! BANG! BANG! The prisoners were not at all happy.

But the children had gone off to rescue Smudge from the hold.

"I'm not coming out," he grinned. "*You've* got to come in!"

"Surprise!" cried Smudge, showing them all the food. And they sat down and began to eat – and eat and eat and eat.

6. The Bun Gun

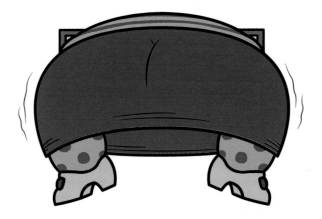

There were eight very cross pirates locked in Patagonia Clatterbottom's cabin. Fifi Foh-Fum tried to escape through the window, but she got stuck too. All you could see was her big wobbly bottom and her little legs, kicking. So that was where the pirates stayed for the rest of the night.

In the morning, the children returned to Patagonia's cabin. Three of them had swords, but Ziggy was pulling a small cannon and holding a bulging sack.

"We will let you out," Corkella called through the keyhole. "But don't dare try anything. You are all going to walk the plank."

They opened the door. Out came Two-Tooth Charlie and Lily Lollop. Out came Patagonia and the teachers. That left the two fattest pirates stuck inside.

"I know how to get Fifi out of the window," said Little Flo. She got a pin and stuck it in Fifi's bottom.

Eeeeeek!
SPLASH!

"I think we'll have to leave Boris until he's thinner," said Smudge. "Now then, you podgy pirates, get up on the gangplank."

And it wasn't long before Lily Lollop and Two-Tooth Charlie joined Fifi in the water, swimming round and round.

Oh look – he can fly! Urgh! Oh no, he can't!

Ziggy grinned at Patagonia and the teachers. "We shall only let you go if you promise to give us better food from now on," he said.

"Scuttle my grommets! Never!" cried Patagonia.

"In that case I shall have to shoot you with my special cannon."

"You wouldn't dare!" said Patagonia fiercely.

"Yes I would," laughed Ziggy, taking aim. "This is my bun gun."

"Boiled barnacles! There's no such thing as a bun gun!" scowled the head teacher.

"Yes there is. It fires buns," Ziggy explained.

BANG!!

"Wobbling whelks! Look at the mess you've made! You horrible shrimp!"

"Give us proper food from now on," Corkella repeated severely.

"Never!" cried Patagonia.

BANG!!!

"Now he's got all of us," complained Miss Fishgripp. "For pity's sake, give in."

"Never!" roared Patagonia yet again.

"Load up the special ammunition," ordered Ziggy.

7. Time For a Bath

"What a horribly messy-looking bunch of pirates," said Corkella. "I think they need a bath, don't you?"

"Yes!" yelled the others. "Put them on the gangplank!"

So Patagonia and the teachers joined the other pirates in the sea. Jazz jumped in too, but that was because he liked getting wet.

"All right," spluttered Patagonia. "We'll feed you properly. Now get me out. I'm cold and wet and I've got jam in my hair."

As for the Woppagobs, they had to
swim to their rowing boat and go away
with nothing, not even their chief,
Boris, who stayed stuck in that hole for
three weeks.

The children celebrated all day. The teachers sulked in their cabins, even though the children offered them some tea.

"How about a nice jam doughnut?" asked Smudge.

"I never want to see a jam doughnut again," growled Patagonia Clatterbottom.

CHOMP! CHOMP! CHOMP!
GLUG! GLUG! GLUG!

Was that a sound effect? No – it was real!